HOW IT WORKS...
THE CAMERA

by DAVID CAREY

with illustrations by
B. H. ROBINSON

Ladybird Books Loughborough

What is a camera?

Of course, everybody knows what a camera is. It is a black box with a small circular piece of glass in the front and a film inside. You point it at something, press a button and when the film is finished you take it to a chemist or photographic shop. In a few days' time, there are your pictures; some good, some not so good and perhaps some that are blurred and hazy.

Now, why were the good pictures good, and others not so good? Why were one or two of them out of focus? What happens in the black box and when the film is being developed? This book will tell you what a camera really is, and, by explaining just how the various parts do their job, help you to make a success of a very interesting hobby. Whether you have a simple camera, an expensive miniature or a cine-camera that takes motion pictures, you can enjoy it just as much.

All normal cameras, however cheap or expensive, have the same basic parts and work on the same set of principles. They consist of a light-excluding body, a lens to give sharp picture definition, and a shutter to let in the light when required. They also have a film winding mechanism, a release to operate the shutter and a viewfinder you look through to see the subject you are photographing.

shutter release

viewfinder

film wind

lens

The pin-hole camera

Actually, the simplest form of camera has few of the features mentioned. It is known as the pin-hole camera. Although not practical for everyday photography, pictures can be taken with it. You could make one at home.

You will need a rectangular box – an Oxo carton will do. Different sized boxes can be obtained to take different films. Cut a hole in the bottom of the box and line the inside with black paper, or you can paint the sides black if you prefer. Next, take a piece of opaque material like tin foil used for cooking, and trim it to fit over the hole you have cut. Stick it down with adhesive tape. With a fine needle or pin pierce the centre of the foil. You can make a shutter from a strip of adhesive tape with a pad in the middle to cover the pin-hole.

Obtain some film from a photographic supplier and, in a darkened room, fix a piece inside the box lid with the emulsion side (dull) towards the camera front. Put the lid tightly on the box, taping round the edges if necessary.

Your camera is now ready for action. Put it on a table facing a window, unstick the shutter and leave it off for a good fifteen minutes before sticking it back in place again. Take the film out, in the dark, wrap it up carefully in lightproof paper and take it to be developed. When you get it back you should have a picture of the view through your window.

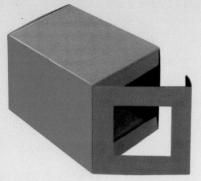

cut a hole in one end and blacken the inside

tape on foil, pierce and position shutter

trim a little off inside flaps of other end

<u>inside darkroom</u>
insert film, close lid and tape

THE COMPLETED CAMERA

How the picture was made

When you placed your camera facing the window and opened the shutter, rays of light coming through the window met the front of the camera. Most of them were dispersed, but one ray from each part of the scene being photographed was able to pass through the pin hole and strike the film. Light can only travel in straight lines, so the rays from the top of the scene would strike the bottom portion of the film, and those from the right would strike the left of the film, and so on. The complete image on the film is, therefore, upside down and the wrong way round. To get a picture that is the right way round, the image on the film, or negative, must be transferred onto photographic paper. (See Page 30).

Because the pin hole is so small, very little light is able to get through it, and that is why an exposure of several minutes is necessary to produce an image on the film. It means that the camera and the subject being photographed must remain perfectly still for quite a long time. If the hole is made larger to shorten the exposure, too many rays of light will enter the camera and a blurred image will result.

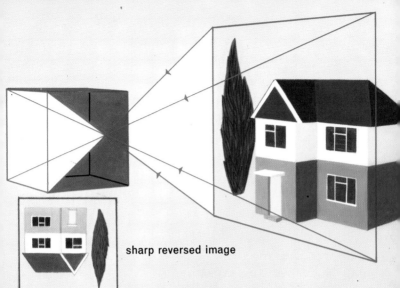

sharp reversed image

HOW THE IMAGE IS FORMED BY A PIN-HOLE CAMERA

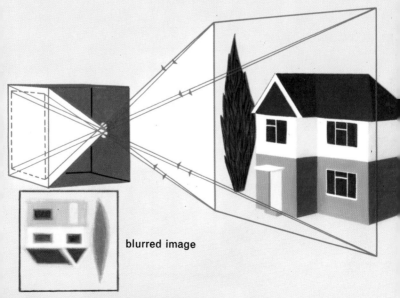

blurred image

THE IMAGE FORMED BY A CAMERA WITH A LARGER HOLE

Light

It is already obvious that light is all-important in photography, and to help us understand the workings of a camera we must know more about light.

Light waves travel in straight lines and can be reflected. A submarine's periscope reflects the light from an object on the surface of the water into the eye of an observer in the vessel below. Light can also be bent, or *refracted*, by passing it through a prism. This is the basis of lens design as we shall see in the next chapter.

Just as it can be reflected, so light can be absorbed, and our ability to see objects depends on the amounts of light they reflect or absorb. Light objects reflect more light than they absorb and are, therefore, easier to see than dark objects. This is particularly true at night when there is not much light about. We 'see' colour because 'white' light is in fact made up of many different colours of light, and when this 'white' light falls on a coloured object, some of its component colours are 'absorbed' by the object and the rest are reflected into our eyes, thus giving us a sensation of colour.

Light is also capable of being filtered so that certain of its component colours are absorbed, while others are allowed to continue on unhindered, once more giving us a sensation of colour.

Photography is nearly always concerned with light that has been affected either by reflection, refraction or absorption; hardly ever with the source of light itself. Few people try to photograph the sun or an electric light bulb!

LIGHT WAVES

the shoebox experiment

LIGHT WAVES TRAVEL IN STRAIGHT LINES

LIGHT CAN BE REFLECTED

LIGHT CAN BE BENT (REFRACTED)

LIGHT CAN BE ABSORBED

LIGHT CAN BE FILTERED

The lens

A pin-hole camera is not practical because a long exposure is necessary to allow sufficient light to pass through the tiny hole at the front. A larger hole admits more light but produces a blurred image. How then can we get enough light for a short exposure and control it to give us a sharp image on the film? The answer is, by using a lens.

Light travels through the air at 186,000 miles every second. Glass is more dense than air, so light travelling through glass is slowed down and its direction of travel is changed, i.e., the light is refracted.

If we take a prism and send a single ray of light through it from a given source, the ray enters at an angle to the side of the prism. It is refracted as it passes through the glass and emerges from the other side of the prism at the same angle at which it entered. If we now put two prisms base to base we will have two rays of light from the same source, one passing through the upper prism and one through the lower prism. Both rays of light enter, are refracted and leave at identical angles so that they come together again at the other side.

A lens is formed by a single, circular piece of glass scientifically ground into a series of tiny prisms.

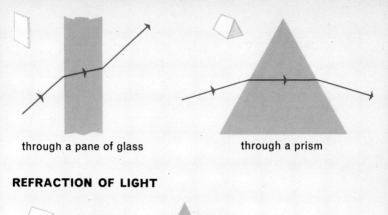

through a pane of glass   through a prism

REFRACTION OF LIGHT

two prisms
base to base

A lense can be thought of
as being composed of many prisms

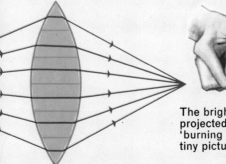

The bright spot of light
projected by a
'burning glass' is a
tiny picture of the sun

Light and lenses

With a lens fitted to the front of a camera, we can let in more light and if a film is placed at the spot where the light rays meet after passing through the lens, we will get a sharp image. The distance between the lens and the meeting point of the rays from a distant object is known as the *focal length* of the lens. Where the rays meet is the *focal point*.

Lenses are ground to give a particular focal length which cannot itself be altered. Light has to enter the lens at a certain angle if the rays are to meet on the film, and this angle is determined by the distance of the lens from the scene or subject being photographed. Rays of light are sent out from every point of the subject and, after passing through the lens, converge on the film in the form of a cone. If the subject is the correct distance away, the rays will meet at the point where the film is placed and a sharp image will result. But if the subject is too far or too near, the rays will meet either in front of the film or beyond it, and instead of sharp points of light striking the film it will be covered in tiny circles of light giving an indistinct and blurred effect. (See diagram opposite).

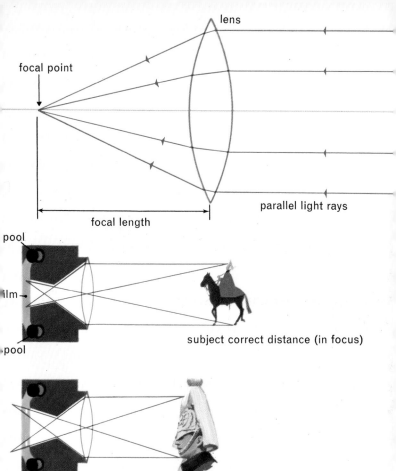

lens

focal point

focal length

parallel light rays

pool

ilm

pool

subject correct distance (in focus)

subject too near (out of focus)

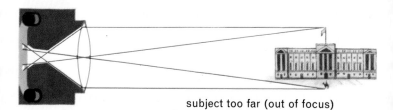

subject too far (out of focus)

Focusing and f-numbers

Simple cameras are fitted with a small fixed-focus lens, and although they are made to give the sharpest picture at a subject-to-camera distance of about 5 metres, they will give passable results as close as 1.5 metres or as far away as, say, 30 metres. This is because angles at which the rays of light enter the small lens do not vary very greatly over these distances. The pictures are blurred but not noticeably so.

The fixed-focus arrangement does not work with more expensive cameras fitted with big lenses. In these it is necessary to provide a method of moving the lens forward or backward in order to vary the lens-to-film distance for different subject-to-camera distances. This is normally done by revolving the lens mounting on a built-in screw-type thread.

Besides having a certain focal length, a lens is also given an f-number. This indicates the size of the lens aperture in relation to its focal length.

$$\text{f-number} = \frac{\text{focal length}}{\text{diameter of aperture}}$$

The smaller the f-number, the bigger the aperture, i.e., f-2·8 is bigger than f-5·6. In the better cameras, lenses can be adjusted to any one of several f-numbers according to the light conditions by means of an *iris diaphragm*. The aperture can be *opened* (made bigger) on a dull day or *stopped down* (made smaller) in bright sunshine.

images close together

lens

HOW A SMALL FIXED-FOCUS LENS PRODUCES CLEAR IMAGES OVER A LARGE RANGE

objects far apart

AN INEXPENSIVE CAMERA WITH FOCUSING LENS

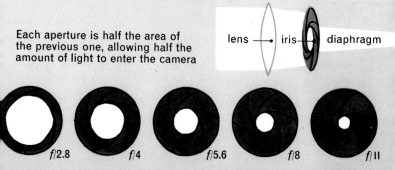

Each aperture is half the area of the previous one, allowing half the amount of light to enter the camera

lens → iris → diaphragm

f/2.8   f/4   f/5.6   f/8   f/11

Shutters and exposures

Lenses, because of their intricacy and the accuracy involved in their manufacture, are the most expensive single part of any camera. Simple cameras have small, uncomplicated lenses so they are cheap to buy. At the other end of the scale, there are cameras costing hundreds of pounds fitted with big, complex lens systems comprising several different types of lenses working in conjunction with one another. You pay your money and you take your choice.

The next most expensive item in a camera is the shutter. This is a device, mounted behind the lens or within a series of lenses, for opening and shutting the lens aperture and exposing the film to the light when a photograph is taken. It is operated by a release on the camera body. Here again, you get what you pay for. Simple cameras have simple, spring-operated shutters timed to give one speed and an exposure of between 1/25th. and 1/50th. of a second. Better cameras have *diaphragm* or *sector* shutters consisting of three or five blades made with watch-like precision to open and close together. These shutters can be regulated from the front of the camera to give exposure speeds of one second up to 1/300th of a second and faster.

Shutter speeds and aperture settings are worked together to obtain a correct exposure for any given light conditions.

400mm telephoto

8 element 50mm standard lens

300mm

200mm

85mm

105mm

18mm

500mm

INTERCHANGEABLE LENSES FOR AN EXPENSIVE 35mm CAMERA

shutter release aperture

shield prevents exposure during re-set

actuating spring
shutter spring *released*

aperture open *released*

shutter re-set

OPERATION OF SIMPLE ROTARY SHUTTER

Depth of field

Depth of field is an expression used to describe the distances in front of a camera within which a sharp, well-focused picture can be obtained. If we take A as the point nearest the camera at which a sharp image obtainable and B the maximum range of focus, the distance between A and B is the depth of field. Small lenses and small aperture openings give the greatest depth of field because there is less variation in the angle at which the rays of light enter the lens. Large lenses and wide apertures give shallow depths of field. (See diagram opposite).

Simple cameras need no preparation before taking a photograph: you just aim and 'shoot'. With better cameras there are three things you must first do. You must adjust the lens focus to the correct distance, then open or stop down the lens aperture according to the brightness of the light, and finally adjust the shutter speed to give the right exposure for the aperture setting you have chosen.

The relationship between aperture and shutter speed is all-important. A wide aperture will require a short exposure, a small aperture a longer exposure. Bearing in mind the limitations in depth of field imposed by wide aperture settings, a smaller aperture with longer exposure is usually the better combination. Something like f-16 at 1/50th. sec. is a good average for bright weather conditions.

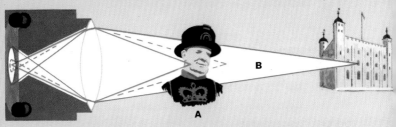

Large 'circle of confusion' (blue) - tower out of focus

LARGE APERTURE - SMALL DEPTH OF FIELD

Small 'circle of confusion' - tower in acceptable focus

SMALL APERTURE - LARGE DEPTH OF FIELD

CAMERA ADJUSTMENTS

The aperture is set at *f*11 and the lens focussed to 5 metres. From the depth of field scale we can see that, at *f*11, the depth of field is from 3 to 10 metres

Film

Whether you use a simple camera or a complicated set of photographic equipment, you cannot take a photograph without film. It is agreed that most amateur photographers take their exposed films to a chemist or other photographic supplier for them to be processed, therefore this aspect of photography is beyond their control. Nevertheless, to understand fully how a camera works we should know something about the material it uses and how that material is treated to give us the object of all our efforts – a picture on paper that we can see.

A black and white photograph is an image in silver. The film consists of a transparent supporting material coated with a mixture of tiny silver salt crystals and gelatine, which together form the light-sensitive *emulsion*. The silver salts make up the operating substance while the gelatine provides a means of holding the crystals together. To the emulsion are added a large number of dyes which make the film respond to different colours, thus giving the various tone values in the final photograph.

Silver salts turn black when exposed to the light and then 'developed'. (See page 28). The negative image on the film will, therefore, be reversed in its light and dark areas as well as in position. Bright portions of the subject which reflect more light will appear dark on the film; dark objects will appear lighter.

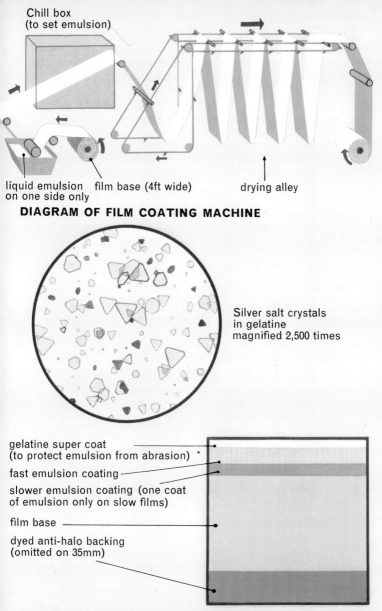

Chill box
(to set emulsion)

liquid emulsion
on one side only

film base (4ft wide)

drying alley

DIAGRAM OF FILM COATING MACHINE

Silver salt crystals
in gelatine
magnified 2,500 times

gelatine super coat
(to protect emulsion from abrasion)

fast emulsion coating

slower emulsion coating (one coat
of emulsion only on slow films)

film base

dyed anti-halo backing
(omitted on 35mm)

CROSS SECTION OF COATED FILM

Loading the camera

Although roll films are available to fit certain types of camera, the great majority of inexpensive cameras bought today are of the film cartridge type. More expensive ones usually take a 35 mm. film cassette.

To load a cartridge it is simply necessary to open the back of the camera, place the cartridge in position in its holder and close the camera again. The winding handle engages in a sprocket on the cartridge and enables the film to be wound into the correct positions for exposing. Numbers printed on the film backing-paper appear through a little window in the camera back to tell you how far to wind for each exposure. Some winding mechanisms are made to stop automatically at the right place.

With 35 mm. cameras the cassette is placed in position and a 'leader' length of film is fed on to an empty spool provided for the purpose. The camera back is closed and the winding mechanism draws the unexposed film out of the cassette and onto the spool. When all the exposures have been made, the film must be wound back into the cassette which can then be removed from the camera and taken for developing.

Your camera must never be opened up once it is loaded because light will immediately 'fog' the film, which will then be spoiled.

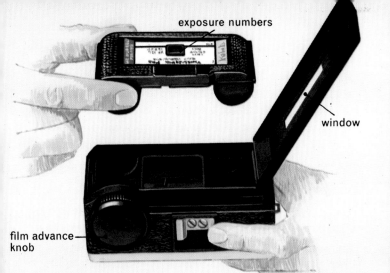

LOADING A 126 MAGAZINE CAMERA

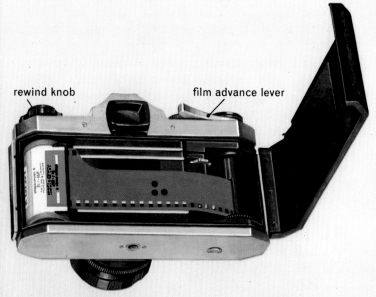

LOADING A 35mm CAMERA

Types of film, speed and grain

A photographer's choice of film is not only one of size or camera loading. There are also different kinds of emulsion which affect a film's speed and its colour-sensitivity, i.e. its ability to reproduce the natural colours of a scene in black, white and varying tones of grey.

All the popular black and white films are *panchromatic* (pan). This means that the emulsion is more or less equally sensitive to all the component colours of white light and, therefore, records the brightness of different colours fairly accurately in tones of black and white.

Films react to light at different speeds. *Fast* films react quickly and are useful for the low light values of winter, dull days and indoor photography. *Medium fast* films give excellent results for all normal purposes, and *slow* films give extra high quality pictures. Film speeds are indicated by their ASA numbers, usually marked on the carton. The greater the ASA number, the faster the film. Of course, film speed must always be taken into account when adjusting the camera's aperture and exposure settings.

Finally we come to *grain*. This is not very obvious on small prints, but becomes apparent in enlargements as a speckled effect on the print. Generally speaking, fast films have a coarse grain; slow films have a fine, less noticeable grain.

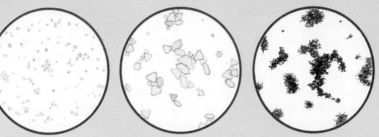

SLOW EMULSION **FAST EMULSION** **FAST EMULSION AFTER DEVELOPMENT**

During the manufacture of fast emulsion the silver salt crystals grow and clump together. If any part is affected by light, the whole clump will darken on development, producing an increase in grain as well as speed.

THE EFFECT OF GRAIN ON ENLARGEMENT x 6 x 64

ASA		
125	50 sec	f22
400	100 sec	f22
800	200 sec	f22

ASA		
125	50 sec	f4
400	50 sec	f5.6
800	50 sec	f8

ASA		
125	200 sec	f2.8
400	200 sec	f4
800	200 sec	f5.6

To minimise grain use the slowest film that will suit camera, subject and light conditions.

Developing the latent image

We have already gained a good general idea of what photography is all about. We have chosen our film and exposed it. Light rays have passed through the lens and affected the film, which now has an invisible image in the emulsion. It is invisible because, even if we could look inside the camera, we should see nothing on the film. This invisible something is known as the *latent image* and we now have to make it visible, i.e. *develop* it.

The chemical solution used to develop the film consists of a rather complicated formula and at this stage of our experience it is not necessary to go into its make-up. All we need to know is that when the film is placed in the developer the chemicals act upon those portions of the emulsion which have been affected by the light. After a certain time the film is removed, rinsed in clean water and then placed in another solution known as the *fixer*. This gets rid of the unwanted silver crystals which have not been affected by the light, leaving only the silver image on the film. Washing and hanging up to dry complete the process.

Compared with the subjects that were photographed, the negative images are reversed. The white portions of the subjects are now black and the original black portions are completely transparent.

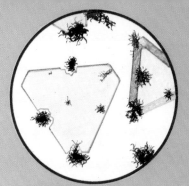

EMULSION DURING DEVELOPMENT
The silver salt crystals are being reduced to metallic silver

EMULSION BEFORE AND AFTER FIXATION

THE SUBJECT AND THE NEGATIVE (COMPARED)

Photographic printing

With the complete film developed we have a strip of rather uninteresting-looking negatives which have to be held up to the light for the images to be distinguished. Because they are all the wrong way round, they must be re-photographed onto paper to obtain positive prints which accurately represent in black and white the coloured subjects that were originally photographed. The process is known as photographic printing.

Photographic papers are made in a similar way to films but the silver emulsion is less sensitive to light. The printing process involves passing light through the negative so that a corresponding image is formed in the emulsion of the paper. This can be done by direct contact of the emulsion side of the negative with the emulsion of the paper. In this method a *contact* print, exactly the same size as the negative, is produced. Another method often used is to project an image of the negative onto the photographic paper through an *enlarger* to produce an *enlargement*.

We now have a latent image on the paper which has to be developed, rinsed, fixed, washed and dried in the same way as the negative.

All developing and printing is done in a *darkroom*. Lighting, if any, is by dull coloured (safe light) lamps which will not affect the emulsions of film or paper.

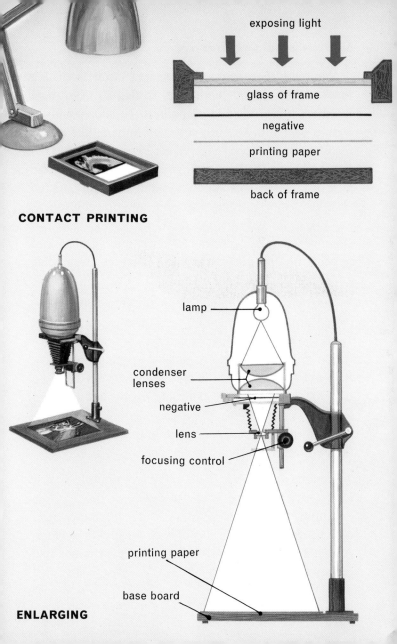

exposing light

glass of frame

negative

printing paper

back of frame

CONTACT PRINTING

lamp

condenser lenses

negative

lens

focusing control

printing paper

base board

ENLARGING

Cameras and cameras

Yes, there are cameras and cameras. Cameras costing three to four pounds and those costing between three hundred and four hundred pounds. Beginners will do well to start with an easily operated camera, like one of the film cartridge or 35 mm. types. These range from the simple varieties with no settings to worry about, like the semi-automatic Instamatic and similar designs, to the cheaper 35 mm. cameras with some aperture adjustment and two or three shutter speeds. There is a wide selection from which to choose in the lower price groups and moving up the scale into the region of twenty-five pounds.

Next we have a range of medium to expensively-priced automatic, miniature, sub-miniature and reflex models. Here again there is a great variation, but they would normally include aperture openings of about f-2·8 to f-16 or 22, and shutter speeds between 1 sec. up to 1/100th, 1/150th or 1/300th sec. They will also have a lens focusing system. These cameras are suitable for the majority of experienced photographers and they can be used under nearly all conditions.

Cameras for experts, both amateur and professional, have a very wide range of aperture and exposure settings, and probably a choice of lenses which are interchangeable to give normal, wide-angle or telephoto facilities. A range-finder or visual focusing arrangement may also be built-in.

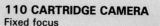

110 CARTRIDGE CAMERA
Fixed focus

2¼ × 2¼ in TWIN LENS REFLEX CAMERA
Built in lightmeter

35mm REFLEX CAMERA
Fully automatic, interchangeable lenses

35mm AUTO-FOCUS CAMERA
Automatic exposure, built in flash

Instant photographs

Sometimes it is useful to be able to see a photograph as soon as possible after it has been taken, perhaps in police work or for newspapers, or to check the exposure when shooting an important picture. With a Polaroid Land Camera a black and white print can be produced in about fifteen seconds, or colour in about one minute.

The camera uses two rolls of film material instead of the usual one. One roll is a paper negative, the other is a special kind of printing paper that is not affected by the light. After each exposure, a tab at the back of the camera is pulled up. This draws the exposed negative and the printing paper between two stainless steel rollers. A small container full of developer in jelly form is attached to the end of the printing paper, and as the two papers pass, in contact with each other, through the rollers, the container is broken and the developer is spread between the negative and printing surfaces. The developing action is very quick, a matter of seconds, and when the printing paper is removed from the camera, there is the picture. A wipe over with a chemically-treated pad and the print is fixed.

Polaroid prints do not always give as good definition as can be obtained from more orthodox cameras, and the negative can normally only be used for the one print. Still, one cannot have everything!

pulling out the film

development for 10-15 seconds

tearing off and peeling the print

fixing

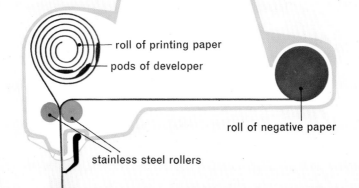

roll of printing paper

pods of developer

roll of negative paper

stainless steel rollers

Colour photography

So far we have considered only the representation of coloured subjects by black and white photography. Colour photography, of course, gives a much more natural effect because we can reproduce on paper or film the scene as we actually see it.

White light is made up of all the colours of the rainbow, or, to be more scientific, of the spectrum. In colour photography all these colours can be reproduced by what are known as the three primary colours of light, i.e., red, green and blue. If we shine a red light, a green light and a blue light onto a screen, we get white light. Yellow light can be obtained by taking blue light away from white light because yellow is the complementary colour of blue. White light minus green light produces *magenta,* a mixture of blue and red light. White light minus red light produces a mixture of blue and green, known as *cyan.* Magenta is complementary to green and cyan is complementary to red. We now have two sets of colours: the primaries of red, green and blue, and the complementaries of cyan, magenta and yellow.

Thus, we can *add* red, green and blue to produce white light, or *subtract* cyan, magenta and yellow from white light to get back to the original colours. Colour photography is mostly concerned with the second, or *subtractive,* process.

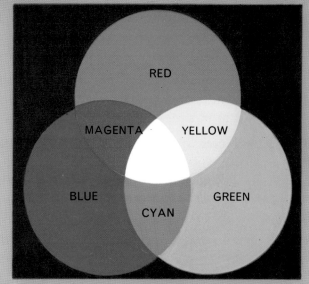

The effect of projecting the primaries onto a white screen:-
The additive process. (Cyan light = white light minus red light).

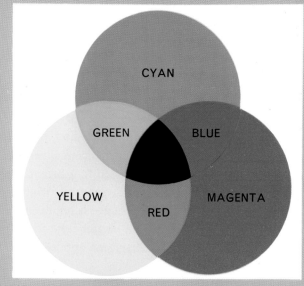

Looking at white light through subtractive filters

The colour processes

There are two main types of colour photographs: colour prints on paper which you look *directly at*, and colour transparencies on film which you project onto a screen or look at in a viewer.

Colour prints need colour negatives. These have three layers of emulsion spread one on top of the other. Blue light from the photographed subject affects the top layer, green the middle and red the bottom. Each layer of emulsion contains a chemical *coupler* which reacts in the developing solution to produce negative dye images: yellow in the top layer, magenta in the middle and cyan at the bottom. The original whites are now black. The printing paper also has three layers of emulsion, each followed by a dye, and sensitive to one colour. During the printing process the yellow, magenta and cyan images of the negative produce positive blue, green and red dye images on the paper to give a faithful reproduction of the original subject.

Film for colour transparencies is again made in three layers, each containing chemicals called *dye formers*. The film is first developed as for black and white to produce a black and white negative image in silver. The remaining silver salts are then exposed to a bright light and placed in a special colour developer. During the following operations the negative image is removed and dye images are formed, which match the colours originally photographed. (See diagrams opposite).

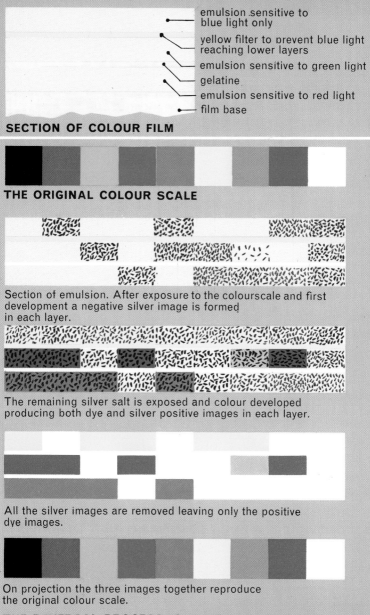

SECTION OF COLOUR FILM

- emulsion sensitive to blue light only
- yellow filter to prevent blue light reaching lower layers
- emulsion sensitive to green light
- gelatine
- emulsion sensitive to red light
- film base

THE ORIGINAL COLOUR SCALE

Section of emulsion. After exposure to the colourscale and first development a negative silver image is formed in each layer.

The remaining silver salt is exposed and colour developed producing both dye and silver positive images in each layer.

All the silver images are removed leaving only the positive dye images.

On projection the three images together reproduce the original colour scale.

THE REVERSAL PROCESS (Colour Transparencies)

Filters

Most of us have taken photographs of a landscape or seaside scene, and while the result has been reasonable from a snapshot point of view, we have somehow failed to get the lovely cloud effects we saw with our eyes. This is where light filters come in. Without going too deeply into their technicalities, it is useful to know something about them.

A filter consists of a piece of coloured glass or gelatine which is fitted in front of the camera lens. All the light entering the lens must, therefore, first pass through the filter. The filter will absorb or take in some colours and will transmit others, that is, allow them to pass through. Colours absorbed by the filter will appear darker on a black and white photograph; those transmitted will be brightened. A yellow filter absorbs its complementary colour of blue and transmits green and red. So to get a good cloud effect use a yellow filter which will darken the blue sky.

The filters used in black and white photography should not normally be used with colour film, unless an unusual effect is required. Because the amount of any component colour or colours of white light can vary – for example, according to the time of day or whether indoors or outdoors – (this is known as a variation of colour temperature), it is sometimes necessary to use colour correction (or c.c.) filters.

Yellow filter, for cloud effects

Orange filter penetrates haze (better than the eye)

Red filter, for special effects particularly light objects against sky. Not suitable for portraits

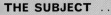
THE SUBJECT ... photographed without filter ... with yellow filter

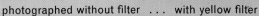
THE SUBJECT ... photographed without filter ... with orange filter

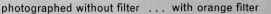
THE SUBJECT ... photographed without filter ... with red filter

Viewfinders, rangefinders and accessories

There is one part of a camera we have so far said little about – the viewfinder. All cameras have some sort of viewfinder to enable you to see the scene or subject you are photographing. In each instance, what you see within the area of the viewfinder you will record on each photograph you take. Cameras held at the waist have a viewfinder with a lens at the front, a mirror to reflect the image upward and a screen on which the image can be seen. Eye-level cameras use an optical viewfinder – in many cases with a 'bright line' frame in which to compose the picture, rather like looking through the wrong end of a telescope.

As photographers become more experienced they usually buy better cameras. They may also use more accessories to help them obtain higher quality pictures. They have a rangefinder with which distances can be accurately measured. This shows two images, one fixed and the other moveable. By means of a focussing mechanism the moveable image can be made to coincide with the fixed one. The correct distance is arrived at when the two images match exactly so that they appear as one.

Other accessories may include flash equipment, an exposure meter to measure the light intensity, filters, lenses to give accurate focussing at short range (for close-ups) and a lens hood to prevent stray light from striking the lens.

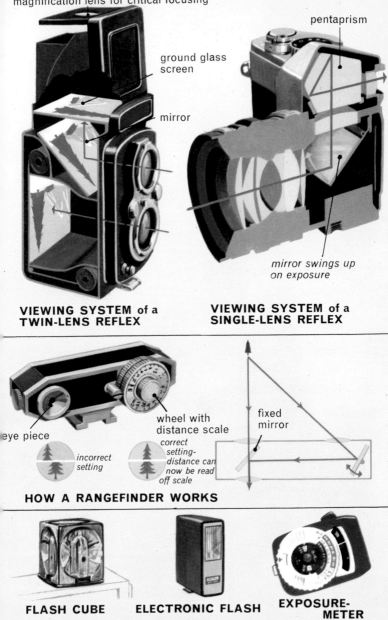

magnification lens for critical focusing

ground glass screen

mirror

pentaprism

mirror swings up on exposure

VIEWING SYSTEM of a TWIN-LENS REFLEX

VIEWING SYSTEM of a SINGLE-LENS REFLEX

eye piece

wheel with distance scale

incorrect setting

correct setting—distance can now be read off scale

fixed mirror

HOW A RANGEFINDER WORKS

FLASH CUBE

ELECTRONIC FLASH

EXPOSURE-METER

Using the camera

It has already been said that there are cameras and cameras, but in the long run a photograph is only as good as the photographer – that's you. Expert photographers can make successful pictures with the simplest equipment, while inexperienced ones can ruin a photograph even though using the most expensive cameras.

With a simple camera it is all quite straightforward. You simply aim and shoot, and so long as the camera and subject are kept perfectly still and the weather is fine and bright, little can go wrong. With better cameras there is more to do: the shutter speed and aperture can be accurately adjusted to give good, bright results and action pictures in not-so-good weather conditions. If you use a filter you will need a wider aperture or longer exposure because the coloured glass absorbs some of the light. For action pictures you will need a fast shutter speed so that you can 'stop' the action and obtain a sharp picture. For given light conditions, a short exposure must be balanced by a wider lens aperture. Fast-moving objects like racing cars and speedboats should be photographed by *panning* the camera, i.e., following the object in the viewfinder and releasing the shutter during the movement. Everything except the object will be blurred but this adds to the effect of speed.

ACTION STOPPED BY FAST SHUTTER SPEED

ACTION STOPPED BY PANNING (THE CAMERA)

The cine-camera

The chief difference between still cameras and cine-cameras is that one takes single photographs while the other takes a series of photographs joined together on a long length of film. In a still camera the film is wound on after each exposure, but in a cine-camera an electrically-operated film transport mechanism drives the film at the required speed to enable exposures to be taken in rapid succession.

Cine-film can be supplied in a self-contained cartridge – a popular system in many modern cine cameras – or wound on to a spool. This is known as the *take-off* spool. Another empty spool is already in the camera waiting to take up the lengths of exposed film. This is the *take-up* spool.

The full take-off spool is loaded into the camera, and the loose end of the film is threaded through the mechanism and attached to the empty take-up spool. Between the two spools is a *gate* consisting of two polished pressure plates, the one facing the camera lens having a rectangular hole through which the film can be exposed to the light. The job of the gate is to hold the film perfectly flat as it passes the lens aperture so that the subject being filmed can be properly focused onto it. Film cartridges work on a slightly different system, but the same principles apply. (See diagrams opposite).

Standard 8 cameras still use the spool system.

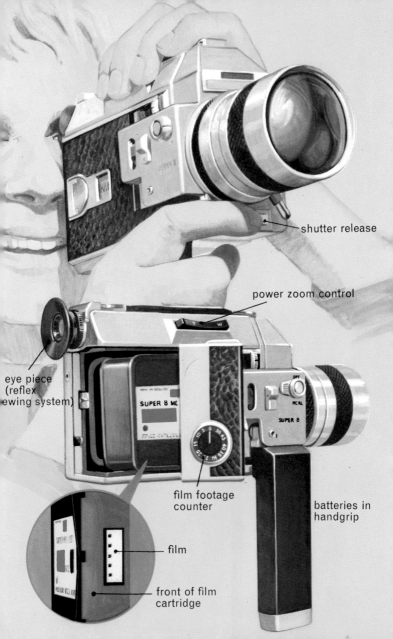

shutter release

power zoom control

eye piece
(reflex
viewing system)

film footage
counter

SUPER 8 M

SUPER 8

batteries in
handgrip

film

front of film
cartridge

How the cine-camera works

Cine-film is divided up into *frames*, and each frame takes a separate image as the film runs through the camera. From what we have already learned about photography we know that film must be kept still at the moment of exposure. Cine-film is no exception, and each frame as it passes through the gate and in front of the lens must be held stationary at the instant of exposure. This is done by a pull-down mechanism consisting of a small hook or claw which engages in a series of holes at the side of the film. While the camera is in operation this hook pulls the film along in a jerking motion, allowing each frame an instant for exposure before pulling it down to make way for the next. This happens at the rate of 18 or 24 frames per second, depending on the type of camera.

A revolving shutter operates in conjunction with the film transport system. It exposes each frame to the light while it is stationary in front of the lens, and obscures the lens while the film is moving during the next pulling down operation.

The electric motor which works the pull-down mechanism also drives the take-up spool or film cartridge. The two are geared to run at the same speed, enabling the film to pass smoothly through the camera.

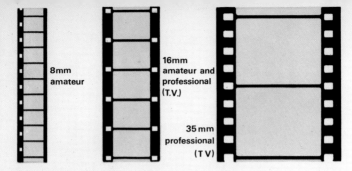

FILM GAUGES COMPARED (ACTUAL SIZE)

8mm amateur

16mm amateur and professional (T.V.)

35 mm professional (T V)

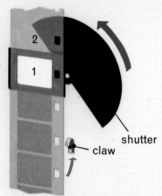

shutter open, frame 1 exposed

shutter

claw

shutter closed, claw engaged in hole

shutter closed, claw pulls down film

shutter open, frame 2 exposed

Types of cine-equipment

Because the shutter of a cine-camera is synchronised with the film frames as they pass in rapid succession through the mechanism, the adjustment of exposure has to be done solely by opening or stopping-down the lens aperture. Small, inexpensive cine-cameras have a fixed-focus lens with only one or two aperture settings. They can, therefore, only be used satisfactorily at certain distances and in good light conditions. The difference between the cheaper and the more expensive cine-cameras depends partly on the size of film they take (8 mm., 16 mm., or 35 mm.), on the type of lens equipment fitted and the refinement of the working parts.

There are variable-speed cameras in which the film can be run at different speeds; normal for natural action shots, fast for *slow* motion or slow for *fast* motion.

Many cameras are now provided with a *zoom* lens, which has largely done away with the need for different lenses to cover long-distance and close-up shots. It can bring the subject nearer or take it further away without upsetting the focus. This system is well demonstrated in television coverage of sporting and other outdoor events.

Photography, still or cine, makes a fascinating hobby. With the knowledge you now have, a camera and practice, you should obtain some very satisfying results.

mm FIXED FOCUS LENS,
anual exposure control

**8mm FIXED
FOCUS LENS,**
automatic exposure
control

8mm 8:1 ZOOM LENS,
automatic exposure control
2 filming speeds

16mm LENS TURRET,
7 filming speeds

Some useful hints when using a camera

A blurred image on a negative probably indicates that the camera has moved during exposure. To avoid this, it is helpful to put the case strap over your head and also wrap it round one or both hands, pulling the strap tight against the back of the neck. Holding the camera in both hands, stand with your legs apart, dig your elbows into your sides and hold your breath at the moment of exposure.

The action of pressing the release button should be one of *squeezing* rather than pressing, thereby avoiding moving the camera downwards. The ideal solution is, of course, the use of a good solid tripod.

When looking through the viewfinder eyepiece, you should see a clear view of the subject you are photographing, but to achieve this the viewfinder eyepiece should be held as close as possible to your eye. This will ensure that you have the correct field of view and enable you to make any adjustments you wish to the composition before taking the picture.

You can determine the distance of the subject being photographed from the camera by measurement, by pacing or by intelligent guesswork, and with a little practice you should be able to estimate correctly. If you pace the distance, you can regard one pace as about $2\frac{3}{4}$ feet.